The Succubus Field Guide

Aspen Thorne

To a very special ace:
You know who you are! Your support through this process was invaluable
and I couldn't have finished without you. I appreciate you dropping
everything to read my rewrites and I love that you think I'm as funny as I do.
Greg is my love letter to you.

To everyone who read my early drafts: You gave me the feedback I needed
to tell this story properly and the confidence I needed to go through with it.
Thank you for coming on this journey with me!

To the asexuals who read this story: Every sex scene is essential
to the plot but there are a lot of them! Greg is only one type of ace
among a rainbow of sexuality. He is the hero in this story because
he is ace, not in spite of it. This story is my love letter to all of
you. The queer community is better because you are in it!

Adventures in Couples Therapy

I t was Gregory's first time seeing a therapist. He didn't know what to expect but he was scared. He heard about psychologists who hypnotized clients to make them believe in aliens and psychologists who convinced folk to electrocute complete strangers for "research". He could remember a dozen other stories about mental health professionals abusing their power except that wasn't what Greg was afraid of. He was afraid his new counselor couldn't help him, and he desperately needed help.

"Hello, Greg?" A slender man with stylish glasses and a funky shirt beckoned him into the next room, "Nice to meet you, Greg, I'm Tim. What brings you to my office today?"

It was awkward at first, but Tim was nothing like Greg expected. He was personable and funny rather than cold and clinical. When introductions were over Greg found himself explaining everything. He was blurting out the entire impossible situation before he could even process his own thoughts. Something about Tim's expression made Greg feel like they were on the same side and the more he spoke the more he wanted to keep talking.

Words poured out of him like water from a bucket and as Greg spoke, Tim listened. He didn't write anything on a notepad or shuffle sheets of paper around, he didn't check little boxes; he just listened. Tim gave no advice and made no diagnoses. Occasionally he would ask a question that made it clear he was following along.

Greg had never felt so...heard. Which was why he told Tim every sordid detail. He talked about the ritual and how Wava began appearing to him soon after. He was surprised to find himself admitting that he joined the ritual to fit in and not for the sexual satisfaction. He even told Tim things he had never said out loud before like how he felt about Sky and even how he felt about sex.

Sex was never that important to Greg. Friendship was far more compelling to him. When his friends got involved in demonology he was interested, too. It was something for them to talk about and study together which was exciting at first. Greg was having so much fun being part of the group that he didn't mind when the study turned to succubi although he only skimmed the material. He liked learning about folklore more than ritualistic details.

Greg didn't take any of it seriously. For him it was about the camaraderie of friends sharing their interests. He was only a little uncomfortable when conversations turned toward rituals. His friends kept discussing how amazing it would be to have a personal succubus to satisfy their desires. They began acting like demonology was more than an interesting field of study. They were acting like believers. Greg just wanted to hang out with his buddies. He knew the last thing he wanted was a personal succubus, but he never thought the ritual would work. He was sure it *wouldn't* work because Succubi aren't real. How could he have known he was wrong?

When he finished speaking Tim looked thoughtful. Greg searched his expression and was surprised to see no hint of judgement in his eyes, "I think we all do things to fit in and it usually works out just fine!" Tim said, "this is a very extreme consequence for going along with the crowd. I think anyone would feel out of control in your situation."

Greg was speechless for a moment, "You just...believe me? You believe that I am being haunted by a succubus that only I can see?"

Tim didn't seem ruffled, "We don't know each other very well but it seems like there are only three possibilities here," Tim lifted one finger, "You are being haunted by a succubus that only you can see," he lifted another finger, "you are having tactile, visual, and audio hallucinations, or," he lifted a third finger and paused for a fraction of a second before finishing, "You are lying."

Greg was almost relieved. He wanted help—needed it—but he wasn't sure if he could accept help from someone who believed in invisible succubi...even though he was being haunted by one. "I'm not lying—" he began but he felt the air in the room heat up. Wava was back. Greg felt his stomach drop. It occurred to him that Tim would surely think he was lying now. Her timing was too perfect.

Tim faded out of his awareness as Wava materialized next to him, "Hello Gregory! How's it going?" She sounded chatty as if she and Greg were comfortable friends. She was naked as always and completely comfortable with her strange and beautiful body, but Gregory still felt secondhand embarrassment. He struggled internally trying to decide where to look. He didn't want to encourage her by staring and he was afraid to reveal how vulnerable he felt by refusing to look. Instead, he froze in place and hoped she would keep her distance. He was quickly disappointed.

"I see you've decided to visit a shrink?" she said wrinkling her nose in exaggerated disdain, "Why? You think I'm not real? You think you need to be locked up or something?" She looked suddenly mischievous, "I wouldn't mind that! We'd have lots of time together," she began to caress herself suggestively, but her mood shifted again and she narrowed her eyes, "I thought you were enjoying our time together!" She frowned, then furrowed her brow, fixing him in her pupil-less gaze, "maybe I just need to try harder."

As she spoke, she walked her fingers playfully up Greg's leg and creeped toward his penis with exaggerated slowness. Greg wasn't in an amorous mood, but it didn't really matter. There was something about Wava that made her irresistible. Even to someone like Greg. He had no interest in sex, but his body responded to her anyway.

She began gently raking her fingertips back and forth along his crotch until his penis started to swell. Greg's cheeks grew hot as he tried to focus on anything else. He should have chosen clothing that would hide an erection better, but it wasn't something he usually needed to think about. Greg tried to focus and remembered Tim was sitting across from him. A wave of shame overcame him as he imagined Tim watching Gregory's cock get hard for no discernible reason. He was going to think Greg was a pervert making up stories to sexually harass therapists.

Wava put her face close to Greg's ear and began whispering breathily, "I love it when you get hard for me," a tsunami of embarrassment engulfed him, but he remained helplessly frozen.

She started increasing the pressure of her fingertips as she stroked his dick over the top of his pants, "When I feel you getting hard my pussy tingles. I want to unzip your pants and take your cock out! I want to lick you and fuck you..."

Dirty talk wasn't really Greg's thing, but it didn't matter. His penis continued to swell until it was throbbing in time with his heartbeat. Wava gripped the shaft of his dick through his pants and started rubbing firmly towards the glans. He felt something warm and impossibly soft on the top of his hand. She was rubbing her naked vulva on him and moaning as he sat motionless, "I want you so bad Greg; I want to rub this pussy on your cock. I want to rub you with my pussy until your cock is dripping with my juices. Then I want you to slide your fat cock inside my pussy and I'll ride you until you cum inside me!" She moved her hips and pushed her clit against his hand while continuing to stroke his penis over his pants.

Greg hated the word 'pussy'. *Pussy, pussy pussy! What a stupid fucking word!* He tried to focus on that, tried to ignore Wava but she was impossible to ignore.

The pants were rough on Greg's skin, but Wava knew what she was doing. Somehow it still felt great. The sensation of her slippery clit rubbing against his hand was overwhelming. Greg struggled to stay present.

"After you cum I'm going to keep stroking your cock with my pussy until you get hard again. Your cock is going to be soaked with both of our juices. It's the perfect time for me to slide your cock up my tight little asshole. You can fuck my ass so much longer and harder, Greg!" She was moaning with pleasure as she spoke.

Greg didn't think of himself as a prude, but he was shocked by her words. Wava could tell and she loved it, "What's wrong? You're not ready to fuck my ass, Greg?" She whispered, "While your cock is deep in my asshole you could use my tail to fuck my pussy. Don't you want to fuck both my holes, Greg? I want you to fuck me so bad! What do I have to do to get you to fuck me?" She continued to stroke him while grinding on his hand. Eventually she managed to get some of his fingers to slide inside of her and they both gasped. Greg out of shock and Wava with pleasure. Wava's excitement was palpable. She hadn't managed to get this far until now.

"That's right Greg, fuck me!" She moaned pushing his fingers further inside her and rocking rhythmically. She was so warm and so wet. It felt ...good inside of her even though he wasn't interested in continuing. He wasn't interested...was he? Wava's nipples slapped gently against his face as she rocked back and forth on his hand. She was becoming more frenzied as her excitement increased. He felt himself wanting to give in. He pictured his lips opening to suck her nipple into his mouth. That was a first for Greg, he had never considered such an activity before. At least not on his own. Not that Greg was a virgin. He'd tried sex before realizing it wasn't for him. Even afterward Greg had done things to please his partners, but he did them in the same way that one might scratch an itch that was out of reach. He didn't relish the activity but he didn't resent it, either.

"Greg!" It wasn't Wava's breathy whisper.

Greg suddenly remembered Tim's presence and his erection faltered. Wava didn't like that. He could see several emotions cross her features before she composed herself. She was angry. Scared?

There was Tim, standing near him now and looking concerned. Wava was still straddling his fingers, squeezing the muscles of her vaginal walls and giving Greg some confusing sensations. So warm and welcoming but not enough to make him forget Tim. Not enough to overcome the embarrassment of having a noticeable erection in front of his new counselor. His dick grew softer.

Wava was visibly annoyed and not bothering to hide it, "I hate fucking when you're distracted. I guess I'm going to have to wait. I won't wait forever, Greg. No matter how many distractions there are." She was gone.

Tim helped Greg calm down and talk about what happened before sending him home, "I'm confident you're not lying about your experience, Greg. I could see that it was very real to you. The next step is to find out if she's a hallucination or magical. I'm giving you a referral to medication management. If the medication works than we have our answer."

NSFW

The medication did not work. Greg stood behind the counter at his job trying not to look at Wava as she stroked his cock with her fingertips and giggled softly. He was talking to a customer and thankful that the counter was between them. He wished she would go away.

"Thank you! Have a nice day," Greg said as the customer finished the transaction.

"Now it's my turn to have a nice day, Greg, you can't keep me waiting anymore," Wava gripped his penis shaft again and held on, increasing pressure rhythmically. He was alone in the store but still very aware that a customer could arrive at any time.

"Unzip your pants, Greg. I'm going to take your cock out and suck it!" Greg wondered if Wava was unable to take that step herself. Maybe if he refrained from undressing she couldn't go further.

"Don't worry Greg, I can do it for you," she said, and he felt his zipper slowly plunge. His heart sunk with it. Seconds later she pressed her face against his crotch, and he could feel her tongue moving his boxers aside to probe for his cock. He wasn't interested in continuing but it didn't matter, his dick was fully erect by the time her tongue found the shaft of his penis.

Another customer entered and began browsing as Wava used her tongue to draw his dick out of his pants. She began licking the glans of his penis in a circular pattern while using her hands to massage the shaft and gently stroke his balls. It would have felt amazing if he wasn't about to pass out with anxiety. If he had wanted it.

Greg was still unsure if Wava was real or a hallucination, but he was fairly certain his dick was fully exposed behind the counter. *Would the customer be able to see? Would he be able to speak? Was he about to be arrested for indecent exposure?*

Wava wrapped her lips around the head of his dick while continuing to circle with her tongue. He couldn't deny it, it felt amazing. She began taking more of his dick in her mouth, bobbing up and down while gasping breathily, "I can tell you like this," she gasped, "It turns me on so much to see you getting horny for me."

The customer approached the counter and panic creeped back. He started to feel the color in the room fade and he slapped his hands into the counter to keep himself present. What would it look like if he passed out now? Fully erect with his naked cock spilling out of his pants. He'd probably wake up in jail and Wava would be there, too. Taking his cock out in front of the other detainees.

He pushed his hips forward to get closer to the counter and hide his naked penis. It had the unexpected effect of forcing his cock further into Wava's mouth. She loved that! She took it all the way to the base and began massaging him with her tongue and sucking more forcefully. She moaned with excitement. Greg did his best to serve the customer. He didn't want to think about how he must have looked or sounded.

When the customer left the store he let out the moan he was holding back. Wava loved it. She was sucking the head of his dick and working the rest with her hands. Periodically she would take his entire penis into her mouth. He felt himself giving in and moving his hips to meet her. Wava was so excited he could feel her body heat rise.

She unbuttoned his pants and pulled them down to his ankles with his boxer shorts. Then she grabbed handfuls of his naked ass to push his cock rhythmically in and out of her throat, "You like face fucking me Greg, don't you?" He couldn't deny it although it wasn't something he would have chosen to do. The fact that she enjoyed it so much made him forget his misgivings. He started to give in to her. He started to participate. He stroked her hair away from her face and caressed her arms as she sucked and licked his cock. She loved that, her moans became louder, and she started sucking and rubbing faster. Her tail whipped back and forth like a cat.

Then she stood up and turned her back to him, leaning over the counter and spreading her legs apart. Her naked breasts flattened against the countertop, and she arched her back so that her ass was pressed against him and her pussy was poised on top of his dick. She felt slick and warm as she rubbed her vulva against his penis. He wanted to thrust his hips forward and penetrate her, but he resisted. Even rubbing against her felt good. Suddenly Greg heard the door open as Wava thrusted against him, guiding his penis inside of her. It felt so good he could tell he was close to cumming already.

Except there was a customer in the store. How did this look? He was standing behind the counter with his pants around his ankles and his penis fully erect and throbbing. Could the customer see, or did the counter hide him? What would it look like if he continued fucking her? Would he be able to pull out or would she stop him? Greg threw himself backwards and hit the floor. Once he was on the ground, he pulled up his pants and zipped them tight, tucking his erection into his waist band to hide it. His skin was still slick from Wava.

He jumped up quickly and saw Wava still bent over the table with her legs spread apart. Her labia were swollen, showing off her welcoming vagina. He could see her vaginal muscles quivering and flexing with desire, "Where did you go?" she sounded genuinely sad, and he felt bad for disappointing her before he reminded himself to keep it together.

He looked beyond Wava and saw his boss standing hesitantly near the sales counter squinting at him. He was thankful for his quick thinking but wondered what she had seen, "You don't look well, Greg," she said.

"That's because you interrupted us just as things started to heat up!" Wava spat petulantly.

"I don't feel well," Greg said, "I've been feeling pretty weird all week." That was the truth.

"Go home then. I can take care of closing up shop!"

A Friend in Need

Greg didn't wait around, he left, but Wava was waiting for him as soon as he sped through the door.

"No one has *ever* resisted me once they are inside of me, Greg. You are the first," she looked stoic, "What am I doing wrong? I *need* you to fuck me Greg. *You* called me here to fuck you! Why would you do this to me?" Wava had tears in her eyes. Greg was shocked to realize he felt guilty. He hadn't stopped to consider her humanity...Demonity? She was a succubus!

"I'm sorry, Wava, I just can't!" he said but she was gone. That was the first time he acknowledged her directly. His instincts told him he needed to resist her. Speaking to her would only let her in. He was starting to question his instincts. Maybe if he let her have her way she would leave. He shook his head, hoping to clear his thoughts.

Greg headed towards his friend Sky's house. The place where it all started. If Sky had a summoning ritual that worked, they *must* know more about Succubi. All of his friends had done the ritual together. His head was swimming with questions. Was Wava appearing to Sky, too. How were *they* handling her? Did Sky know how to send her back? Was any of this even real?

Greg wasn't prepared for what he saw when he entered Sky's home. His friend was upstairs in their bedroom. They were completely naked and didn't seem to notice Greg. Sky appeared to be alone thrusting their hips into the open air but their penis was contorting in ways that couldn't have been independent. It was as if they were thrusting into an invisible person who was thrusting back causing Sky's dick to move unnaturally with each rhythmic thrust.

Greg's anxiety and embarrassment were battling for dominance. He didn't like seeing his friend that way. He tried the grounding exercises he learned from Tim to calm himself and gather his thoughts.

Greg called Sky's name, but they didn't seem to hear him. Sky continued moaning, grunting, and thrusting away ignoring both hand waving and hollering. Their skin was slightly flushed yet paler than usual. Greg thought they looked dehydrated. Had Sky been fucking nonstop this entire time?

Greg considered how angry Wava became at distractions and faltered in his efforts to get Sky's attention. He didn't want to be a nuisance to Sky's demon. Not until he knew what he was dealing with. Perhaps he could find the information he needed by himself.

Greg left the bedroom and searched the house. He didn't have to look far. Wava was sitting on the coffee table when he entered the living room. Her legs were spread apart so far, she was almost in a full split. A book titled "Succubus Field Guide" was lying open on her lap so that Greg would expose her provocatively poised pussy if he tried to take it.

Greg detoured from Wava and grabbed a giant sports drink from the kitchen, trying to look casual. Sky didn't acknowledge him when he returned but they gulped the sports drink when he pressed it to their lips. Their skin lost its grey hue as soon as the bottle was empty. Wava approached him curiously, "You like to watch, Greg? Do you want to see your *friend* fucking Inka, or do you want to see *me* fucking Inka?"

Wava snapped her fingers, and the air became thicker

somehow. Greg's embarrassment grew exponentially as Inka materialized. Sky's dick was thrusting into Inka relentlessly. Her legs were spread wide enough that Greg could see his friend's penis moving in and out of her. Inka's eyes were half lidded but bright and manic. She was gasping and moaning and encouraging Sky to keep going. Sky was like a zombie, pounding and sweating with exertion.

Wava sauntered over to Inka, bent down, and began to kiss her deeply. Inka looked positively delighted. Even Sky seemed to react. The twinkle in Sky's eyes told Greg Sky could see Wava and they were enjoying the view.

Inka didn't waste any time with introductions. She began to massage Wava's breasts with the palm of her hands and her fingertips flickered expertly over Wava's nipples. Sky said nothing but his eyes expressed his pleasure while he pounded into Inka with renewed vigor.

Wava quivered with pleasure and returned Inka's caresses, "I should have known you were a watcher," she gasped toward Greg.

Greg *wasn't* into watching, in fact his cheeks were so hot with embarrassment he felt feverish. Regardless of his feelings he could feel his penis getting hard. *Not again!*

Wava climbed onto the bed and placed a knee on either side of Inka, reaching between her own legs to stroke Inka's clitoris. Sky was enthusiastic about the double stacked Succubi. Their hips brushed against Wava's naked ass each time they thrusted toward Inka. As Wava's fingers stroked Inka's clit Sky pounded tirelessly.

Wava spoke to Greg through a mouthful of Inka's nipple, "Maybe your friend wants to fuck us both, would you like to see that?"

Greg found the idea absurd, but his penis responded anyway. Wava noticed his conflicted expression and smirked,

"Don't be jealous, Greg! I want to fuck you *so bad,* but you keep letting me down. Maybe your friend will let you join us. Inka and I will suck your cock while your friend takes turns spit roasting us."

Inka giggled gleefully, "If *he* doesn't want to fuck you, Wava, Sky and I will fuck you!" her tail flicked toward Wava's labia and lingered suggestively.

Wava moaned with desire and Inka's tail abruptly entered her vagina and began pumping forcefully, "Sky, baby, help me fuck her!" Inka's voice snapped Sky to attention.

They obediently withdrew their dick from Inka's pussy, still dripping with her juices. Wava was already gasping with pleasure as Inka's tail punched into her rapidly. Sky gently probed Wava's anus with the head of their slippery cock, then entered her as she pressed toward their body. Wava moaned louder. Inka continued fucking Wava's pussy forcefully while Sky fucked her asshole with gusto. Inka was also working Wava's erect nipples with her nimble fingers while yelling out encouragement to Sky.

Succubus 101: Making Deals with Devils

Greg would rather put out a fire with his face than witness another moment of their fuck fest, but his cock had a mind of its own. He was uncomfortably hard, and it felt as if his heart was trying to escape through his dick. Throb Throb Throb.

Nevertheless, Wava was distracted, and Greg was determined to use it to his advantage. He slipped out of the bedroom and grabbed the Succubus Field Guide. He searched through it desperately, trying to find something that could help his friend.

It was clear to Greg that Sky would continue fucking Inka until they died of dehydration or exhaustion, whichever came first. He needed to find a way to send the Succubi back home and save his friend.

He didn't have much time with the book before he felt a familiar presence. Wava must have noticed Greg was gone. She entered the living-room and saw him flipping through the Succubus Field Guide.

"Experience is much more valuable than academics," she said dryly, "Why don't you come to the bedroom I'll give you Succubi 101."

Greg ignored her and continued scanning the guide.

"Come on, Greg, what's your deal?" she said, "*You* called *me*! I didn't come here uninvited. Why are you treating me like an evil stepmother?" She paused, "Or is *that* what you're into? Are you a mother fucker, Greg? Cuz you're acting like a mother fucker!"

"Wava, I'm sorry, I can't..." he trailed off as his eyes caught sight of something on the page: Banishment! Too late, Wava closed in and snapped up the book before he could see the spell.

"You can't?" She looked angry but her voice was deceptively soft, "You're trying to banish me?"

Greg said nothing but cast his eyes to the floor and remained still.

"Fine, Greg. Since you're being such a little bitch, I'll *let* you banish me...but *you* have to let me have my way first!"

Greg remained silent, afraid of what she was going to say next. Wava looked at the field guide disdainfully before returning her gaze to him, "I'll even give you the correct spell. This one is complete garbage, just ask Inka and Sky!" She tossed the book to the floor and opened her hand. A scroll materialized with a puff of pink smoke. She held it up, "Do we have a deal?"

Greg didn't look up but whispered, "What deal?"

Wava smiled devilishly, "You make us cum, Greg, and I'll let you use the banishment spell. I'm getting tired of this place, anyway. You're so cute! So much potential, but ugh, what a dud!"

Greg spoke up cautiously, "Who do you mean by 'us', Wava?"

Wava laughed as if Greg just delivered the cleverest of punchlines, "Oh Greg, you keep reminding me why I like you so much! I underestimated you," she scrunched up her face in both amusement and annoyance, "I always think the quiet ones are stupid but you're not stupid, are you?"

"I hope not," he mumbled.

She smiled fondly, "So humble, it makes you even more irresistible. Okay, I'll come clean! I want you to make all three of us cum. Me, Inka…and Sky!"

Greg gasped involuntarily, "Impossible!"

"What's wrong, Greg? Afraid of a little deep throat?" She giggled, "No, you're right, Sky's not *little!*"

"No Wava, that's an impossible deal! How can I make Sky cum after they've been drained by Inka? They're so dehydrated I'm afraid they won't live through the night!" as soon as he said it out loud, he felt the tears he was holding back flowing freely down his cheeks. He was terrified for Sky and furious with himself for giving Wava more leverage. If she wasn't aware of Greg's feelings for Sky before, she knew now.

"I keep underestimating you, Greg," she said, "You're right! I was going to make an impossible deal with you but you're so sweet I can't go through with it," with a gesture she made the scroll disappear, "Here's what I can do: Inka and I will find someone to do for the night and you can help Sky recover some fluids. We'll return tomorrow night, and *you* will make us cum. After that Inka and I will release you and go….that is if you still want us to. This is the best deal you're going to get. If you're smart, you'll take it."

Greg looked Wava in the eyes for the first time and spoke softly, "Can I win this challenge?"

Wava quirked an eyebrow, "It's not going to be easy but yes, smarty pants, you can win," she extended her hand and Greg took it. They shook hands once and Wava was gone. Greg felt like collapsing but he forced his legs to carry him back to Sky.

Excuse Me While I Kiss the Sky

Sky was on their back on the bed, still nude, but no longer erect. Sky's complexion was grey, and their eyes appeared sunken. Sky's body was as flaccid as their penis and Greg could tell they wouldn't be able to stand on their own.

Tears flowed freely down Greg's face as he took in the scene, "We have to get you to a hospital!"

Sky croaked weakly, "No…" then a little stronger, "I'm okay…I just need… some water. I…I'm so sorry, Greg, I didn't know…"

Greg cut them off, "It's okay, Sky, none of us did."

"How…" Sky began but Greg shook his head.

"It's not over," he said, "I made a deal with Wava."

Greg brought Sky something to eat and drink and told them about the deal, "I'm so sorry Greg," Sky began but Greg stopped them.

"Let's not waste our time on apologies. Inka and Wava are coming back tomorrow night. I need to make all three of you cum to get them to release us. That includes *you* and I'm not a succubus. I can't make you cum if you don't rehydrate and rest."

Sky's blush brought some healthy color back to their face and sent waves of relief through Greg's body. He was finally able to relax his tense muscles and drape himself across the bed next to Sky, "I thought they were going to kill you!" he said.

Sky reached out a hand and laid it on Greg's back comfortingly, "I'm sorr—I mean, I'm glad you came to my rescue."

Greg turned to face Sky and realized how close their lips were to his, "Me too," he said lamely and Sky grinned.

"Greg," Sky said hesitantly, "I know you're not into relationships or whatever, and I'm not saying this to make you feel obligated or any kind of way, but I have...uh...I have the biggest crush on you and you don't have to—" Greg's laughter cut them off.

"Sky, I'm not laughing at you..." he said between guffaws, "I mean I *am* laughing at you but it's..." Sky waited patiently for Greg to control his hysterical laughter, "I'm *so* into you, Sky, you're all I think about..." he paused, "and it's not relationships I'm not into, it's sex. I don't hate it; I just don't care for it...you know?"

Realization dawned on Sky's face as they realized how hard Greg must have fallen to summon a succubus and *not* be interested in sex. They leaned closer to him and whispered, "How do you feel about kisses?"

Sky let Greg close the distance and press his lips to theirs. He felt like he'd been electrified; his entire body tingled as they locked lips. They stayed like that for some time before Greg pulled back, "We should save it for tomorrow. You need your rest."

Sky rested on his elbow looking like the cat that got the cream before suddenly furrowing his brow, "Greg how are you gonna...you know..."

"Make you cum?"

"Uh, yeah...if you..."

"Don't like sex?"

"Yeah...how is that going to work?"

24

Greg grinned, "I don't care for it, that's true, but I'm actually pretty good with my tongue...and my hands...and my dick to be honest," he said, trying to be nonchalant and hoping his embarrassment wasn't showing through his bravado.

Sky looked away so Greg couldn't read his expression, "It's not going to be...bad for you, right?"

Greg gave them a comforting squeeze, "Not the part where I make you cum but yes, Sky! This whole situation is terrifying!"

Sky turned their face back to Greg, their eyes were welling with tears and mixture of emotions, "I'm sorr—I mean *thank you.* Thank you for saving me with your manly sexual prowess."

Greg fell asleep with Sky nestled in his arms. They slept well into the afternoon and woke up feeling refreshed in spite of everything.

"There's something we need to talk about," Sky said as they ate a cozy brunch together.

"What is it," said Greg, lost in Sky's brown eyes.

"You can't cum tonight," Sky said with a frown, "this is usually the last advice I'd give to a partner but I'm certain we'll lose if you cum."

Greg listened patiently and Sky continued, "When I was with Inka I was... uh, *mostly*, in control of myself until she made me cum for the first time. After that it was like her power over me increased and I belonged to her. Every time I came, I felt her power grow as I became weaker. I knew I was going to die fucking her and I didn't care. I wanted to keep giving her my life force. If you cum tonight, it's over. We will both die."

Greg nodded, "I suspected as much," he said, "Wava has power over me. She's hard to resist. I *want* to give her what she wants. I actually penetrated her at work!"

Sky laughed uproariously, "I can't imagine that! Holy shit does the store have security cameras?"

Greg paled, then nodded, "Yes, my boss never checks them though and we record over the same tape so hopefully I still have a job when this is over. Other people can't see her so I can only imagine what that looked like!" He shuddered, "Anyway, I could tell Wava was being tricky when she said they would go 'if I still wanted them to'. I know I'm ace but my dick seems to forget that when she's around. I'll do my best, it's all I can do."

"Don't cum for me baby!" Sky said in a ridiculously sultry voice then leaned in for a smooch. They both dissolved into laughter.

Nightfall came too soon for Greg. He and Sky spent the day in the dreamy state of new lovers. He almost succeeded in forgetting what was in store for them. As the sky grew dark so did Greg's anxiety. Unbidden thoughts started rising to the surface of his mind and he rested his face on Sky's chest and breathed in their scent.

"This isn't my ideal situation for our first time," he said brushing his fingers lightly over Sky's bare skin.

"Oh?" Sky said in mock surprise, "what *is* your ideal situation? You know other than never having sex, right?"

Greg looked up at Sky's face, "No, I don't mind the occasional sexing when I'm dating," he said, "It's not really my thing but it's like taking part in my partner's hobby. I don't really get it but I understand for some it builds intimacy and closeness and they need it sometimes."

Sky nodded, "I get it, it's like how I feel about heavy metal. I can appreciate the artistry, I can even enjoy it with my metal friends, but I just don't love it enough to make a metal playlist."

Greg laughed, "That really is how I feel!" and then he started to cry.

Sky held him closer and said nothing for awhile. They were having their first discussion about their sex life as a couple, and they were heading to their sexual doom. What was there to say?

"I can still fuck other people, though, right?" they finally said.

Greg was laughing and crying, "Yes! Please do! I could never keep up with you!"

"Okay but I won't summon anymore demons I'll go on grinder or tinder or something."

"Thank you, that's all I ask!"

What's a B J Between Friends?

And then Wava was standing next to him, smiling radiantly, "It's time! Time for my little bitch to make me cum!" She said grandly spreading her arms.

Inka materialized a fraction of a second later and snapped her fingers. Sky moved fluidly to her side and immediately straightened to attention, "Hello my little whore, I missed you!" She said, sounding genuinely affectionate. Sky said nothing but the glimmer in their eyes was adoring.

Inka pointed her finger at Sky and their clothes slid rapidly off their body with a faint trace of red steam. Then she reached down and cradled their balls, gently tugging and rubbing until their dick was at half-mast.

"Don't make it too easy on him!" Wava said but she didn't sound too concerned.

"Oh, that's right!" Inka said, "You should be the one to get Sky baby hard. Mmm, I like that idea."

"Me too!" Wava agreed, "There's something delicious about watching a friend suck his buddy's cock for the first time. I'm getting wet thinking about it."

Wava's demeanor was bolder and more dominant. She assumed she held all the cards, and she was letting Greg know it. He caught himself relishing the fantasy of Wava eating humble pie after discovering she was underestimating him again. He tried to keep his ego in check: sudden confidence would raise suspicion. Greg wanted Wava to relax and trust that she had this challenge in the bag. He needed her to keep believing she couldn't lose so she would cum for him.

Greg realized that Wava didn't know what had transpired between himself and Sky. As far as she knew Sky was just a buddy and Greg had never sucked a cock. He decided to take advantage of her ignorance. He needed to make Sky cum last in order to make Inka and Wava comfortable enough to do it first.

Greg got down on his knees gingerly, visibly shaking. He didn't have to fake his nervousness and embarrassment. Greg was an ace champion cock sucker, but he never had an audience before. His face was crimson as he sidled reluctantly toward Sky's dick. He reached out as if it was an actual trouser snake ready to bite him.

Inka and Wava snickered as they encouraged him, "Come on Greg, grab it like this!" Inka said gripping Wava's tail suggestively.

"Stroke it like this!" Wava said expertly running her fingers up and down Inka's phallic tail, causing her to moan with pleasure.

"Lick it like this!" Inka moaned, seeming to forget who the performance was for as she plunged Wava's tail down her throat and withdrew it to tease with her tongue. Wava gasped with pleasure and started throat fucking Inka. Greg was disappointed to notice his dick getting hard as Wava moaned, plunging her tail down Inka's throat over and over. He wasn't normally into watching but the two succubi had an irresistible sexual energy. Maybe he was the one underestimating *them*.

Wava and Inka must have misinterpreted Greg's deer in the headlights stare as they laughed in delight! "It's okay, Greg, maybe you can start with us!" Wava laughed.

"Get warmed up with my sweet pussy" Inka giggled seductively, spreading her labia with her fingers to show off her glistening clit. It looked like it would taste like strawberry shortcake. Greg licked his lips involuntarily which sent a shocking thought running through his mind: *I'm going to die eating strawberry shortcake pussy.*

Greg felt his panic continue to rise, sending his dick in the opposite direction. He felt like he was floating way from his body and witnessing events from above. His breathing became frantic, and Wava's voice sounded like it was under water, "Whoa, it's okay Greg! Use that thingy Tim said..." she trailed off, unsure of what came next, having not been paying attention to Tim in therapy.

Greg *had* been listening, Tim showed him an easy grounding exercise, but he'd never tried it before. He desperately started saying the names of things he saw, "Lamp, sheet, desk... laptop...uh...lamp. I already said lamp...uh strawberry shortcake clit," he said, and a fresh wave of panic rose in his throat, bubbling out as a frenzied laugh. Inka laughed with him which had an unexpectedly calming effect.

"You know it might taste like strawberry shortcake," Inka said, "Why don't you let Sky have another Gatorade and come find out! I worked them pretty hard last night," her voice was comforting, it sounded deceptively familiar. It sounded like a voice he could trust. Were they playing good cop bad cop?

It didn't matter, he needed to make all three of them cum. He might as well start by eating Inka's pussy, regardless of its resemblance to a favorite dessert.

A Power Bottom to Rule Them All

Inka's pussy was indescribably delicious. It did not taste like shortcake but there was a sweetness, and it did feel like dessert. Greg tried to focus; he knew he had a chance to get her to cum before she could stop herself if he moved fast enough. Years of quickies to get his partners off were going to be tested today. He would try to make her cum without using his dick. He wasn't sure how long he could last if he penetrated her.

Greg started off clumsily, leaning into his schtick, licking between her labia but barely brushing his tongue against her clit. He took advantage of his feigned ineptitude to grab onto Inka's tail and hold it awkwardly. He used his tongue to probe lightly around her clit while not doing much of anything with the rest of her. Wava called out encouragement, praising him for his efforts as if putting his tongue between her pussy lips was a showstopper.

Before Inka could register the sudden skill Greg opened his mouth and buried his entire face into her, circling and flicking his tongue across her clit rapidly. As he did so he plunged her phallic tail into her vagina, angling it upward to hit her G-spot and pumping it with expert pressure. Inka fell right into his trap. She came long and hard, squirting a stream of warm liquid onto his chin and chest. Afterward she remained prone, panting with satisfaction and shock.

Greg looked up in time to see Wava's smirk turn into a sneer before she could compose herself. He used Sky's blanket to dry the liquid from his chin and hoped Wava believed in beginner's luck. Maybe she would think Inka's orgasm was a fluke. He searched her expression and felt his heart skip a beat. The look on Wava's face told Greg there was a punishment coming.

"What a good little bitch, you are, Greg!" Wava said, lacing her tail between her own legs and placing it against her like a strap on. Greg was already prone but still fully clothed, face resting between Inka's thighs. Wava placed her hand on the back of Greg's neck and squeezed lightly, letting him feel her sharp claws. He could feel the tip of her tail pressing against him as she crouched, "You're such a giver, Greg! I think I should let you receive for once," she said sweetly, "as a reward."

Her voice was sweet but menacing and Greg was aware that Wava was about to fuck him in the asshole but *not* as a reward. This was a punishment for making Inka cum so quickly. Greg was no stranger to anal, but he had much less practice in that arena. He planned on relying on the element of surprise, yet again, but it would be tougher to pull off this time.

Wava released Greg's neck and drew her claw down his back softly. As she did Greg could hear the fabric of his shirt tearing away. She was showing off how sharp her claws could be, and Greg was sufficiently intimidated as his shirt fell to the ground in tatters. He spared a glance at the ruined shirt and felt a twinge of disappointment. He had borrowed it from Sky. *Oh well, there would be other shirts to borrow. Sky was a clothes horse.*

Wava's claw reached the waistband of his jeans, and she hooked her finger underneath, making a little come-hither motion and slicing through the denim just as easily as she sliced off his shirt. Greg shivered, feeling very vulnerable and very naked in that moment. Wava continued slicing through his pants, cutting them all the way to his asshole, and lingering there. Greg didn't have to fake the quickening of his breath and he was pleased to feel his skin growing hot and flushed. He was giving Wava exactly what she wanted, he was terrified.

Greg had an ace up his sleeve, so to speak. He observed that the succubi tail ends were just as sensitive as their sexual organs and he saw ridges along Wava's tail that would slide against her clit as she fucked him. Greg remembered how excited Wava got when she successfully turned him on. He had a few moves that might work on Wava even though he was more confident in his cock sucking skills. He was hoping he could take her cock well enough that she would cum before being able to stop herself.

Greg was uncomfortably aware that he risked giving away his hand if the maneuver didn't work. There would be no question that Greg had experience taking cock after this. Wava wouldn't believe his little show with Sky. Which meant that both Succubi were going to do their best to get Greg to cum before Sky did. If he couldn't make Wava cum now it was over. There was no way he could hold back his orgasm with two demons doing their best to pleasure him. He needed to pull out all the stops.

Greg glanced over at Sky and almost laughed when he saw their rock-hard erection. They were clearly enjoying what they saw. Of course, all Sky needed to do was cum. For the first time in his life Greg was relieved that his partner was an insatiable slut. Knowing how much Sky was enjoying this gave him the boost he needed to perform for Wava.

Greg's shredded pants hit the floor and he shivered with anticipation. Wava inserted her tail into her own vagina and withdrew it, slick with her juices and ready for Greg's asshole.

She placed her tail back into position and crouched over Greg once more. He could feel her tail pressed lightly against his naked asshole as she reached down and cupped his balls, squeezing just a tad too tight, and using them to guide his hips up and into position, "Good boy!" She said when his ass was pointed skyward with his back arched toward the floor.
Wava's tail cock probed Greg's anus lightly and Greg went all in.

He opened himself up to her by relaxing his anal muscles then bearing down. Next, he pushed his body backward for a flawless entry and moaned like a whore. His dick was fully erect.

Wava ate it up. She gasped with pleasure and delight, grabbing a handful of Greg's hair, and pulling his head slightly back as she fucked him. Greg let a shiver roll down his spine then pumped his hips in a serpentine motion, massaging Wava's tail cock with his asshole. He increased his undulations causing his balls to rock back and land against Wava's body. She thrusted harder to match Greg's rhythm and he clenched down on her each time she pushed forward, inviting her deeper each time.

Greg moaned in time with Wava's thrusts and rolled his back in a way that drove his past lovers wild, "Yes! Yeah! Oh yes! Please..." he moaned, knowing exactly how to sound to get his lovers to cum quickly. Wava seemed like the type that would want to cum with him. He needed to convince her that he was about to cum without actually climaxing.

Faking excitement had the unfortunate effect of increasing Greg's actual excitement. He tried to focus on something else. Something that could keep him from falling under the succubus spell without sending him into a panic attack. He remembered fucking one of his first boyfriends like this. Greg made him cum instantly when he stroked his own cock by pushing it back between his legs and rubbing it against his partner's balls. It reminded Greg of milking a cow at the time and completely took him out of the moment. Thankfully his boyfriend never noticed, and the maneuver became a favorite. He hoped he could try it with Wava and make enough fuss for her to think he was cumming and cum with him.

Greg balanced his weight on his elbows and lifted his hips to envelope Wava's cock greedily, gasping with pleasure as he did. He pressed his ass against her skin and clenched down on her cock pulling it forward just enough to let her know he was *giving* her control. He could drag her by the cock if he wanted to. Before she could fully register that her cock belonged to him, he made his move. Greg balanced the bulk of his weight on one elbow to liberate his dominant arm. He used the free arm to push his cock and balls between his legs and rub them against Wava.

"Oh Wava, oh yes" he moaned, inserting a desperate note into his voice. He allowed his breath to become more frenzied and began clenching his asshole rapidly, trying to mimic the involuntarily movements of an orgasm, "Yes! Fuck me! I'm cumming!"

"Oh Fuck!" he heard Wava gasp, and he knew she was cumming in that moment. The wave of relief and joy nearly made Greg cum with her for real and he did his best to picture awkward cow udders as he rubbed his dick onto her. Wava pumped forcefully as she came, and Greg was thankful for his ridiculous visual when he felt hot liquid releasing from her tail cock and filling him up. He almost came again; the feeling was surprising and sensual. He had no idea she could ejaculate from her tail.

"Greg," Wava gasped, withdrawing her tail from his asshole, "I had no idea you were a *power bottom!*" She gave his ass a playful slap as she spoke then bent over and unexpectedly licked his asshole, savoring the taste of her own ejaculate. It continued to leak from his body, running down his thighs and dripping onto the floor. There was so much cum oozing from him it was impossible to tell that Greg faked his orgasm. Especially since his cock was in position to be covered by Wava's cascade of cream when she reached climax.

Throne of Sky

"**L**ooks like there's only one thing left to do!" Inka exclaimed, excited to involve her plaything. She snapped her fingers and pointed to the edge of the bed. Sky moved like liquid to fill the spot she indicated. Their dick was hard and throbbing in time with their quickening heartbeat. Greg could see a stream of precum flowing from the tip of their dick. He was once again relieved that Sky was horny and ready even after several nights of gratuitous demon fucking and only one day of recovery.

Greg knew these next moments were critical. He needed to get Sky off and get away before Inka and Wava could make him cum. He needed to mimic Sky's adoring obedience to keep the Succubi complacent. Wava gestured toward Sky and Greg mimicked rapt attention, "Why don't you sit on Sky's cock my little power bottom," she said magnanimously.

Greg moved rapidly to Sky, standing with his legs apart and his ass level with Sky's gaze. He moved forward at the waist, arching his back to emphasize the curve of his buttocks. Sky was practically drooling. Greg used both hands to spread his asscheeks apart, causing more of Wava's creamy ejaculate to leak out and flow down his balls. Greg didn't dare to spare another look at Sky's penis but hoped like hell his aim was true. He bent at the knee and sat firmly in Sky's lap. Thankfully his luck held, and Greg's asshole wrapped Sky's dick like a present.

Now it was Sky's turn to moan like a whore and Inka moaned with him looking at Wava with renewed excitement, "This is the most powerful bottom I have ever seen!" she gushed, adding quietly, "for a human, anyway."

Greg did his best not to swell with pride at the compliment. His skills were heavily focused on getting partners to cum quickly so they could move on to something more interesting. He reasoned that the succubi were probably accustomed to heterosexual men with less experience receiving dick. Inka's admiration was not a good reason to get cocky. He was painfully aware of his greatest weakness: stamina.

"Look at my regal little whore sitting on a throne of Sky!" Wava said, laughing at her own joke.

Sky laughed too, cuing Greg to chime in and giggle along. He gave a little wiggle and clenched down on Sky's penis driving it deeper into himself as he did. He tried not to let the smugness show on his face when Sky's laughter turned to gasps of pleasure.

Too late Greg realized his mistake when Wava's expression darkened and even Inka looked keen. He hadn't been given permission to wiggle. Quick as a flash Inka was kneeling on his left and Wava on his right, "Will you cum for me if I suck your cock?" Wava whispered, not waiting for an answer.

She wrapped her lips around the head of his penis and used her serpentine tongue to penetrate his urethra. Greg had never tried sounding before and he did *not* enjoy the sensation. There was a strange pressure and a slight pain even though Wava's tongue was expertly gentle. He felt like he needed to urinate. Trying to keep his head in the game he feigned pleasure, "Oh Wava," he gasped, "fuck my hole with your tongue! It's so good!"

"Mmmm...you like that, Greg? I'm going to fuck you like you've never been fucked before," Inka whispered delicately into his ear, flexing her fingers while Wava continued penetrating his cock hole. Greg refrained from commenting that he was *already* being fucked like he'd never been fucked before. He tried to focus on clenching and releasing his anus in time with Wava, hoping that Sky would cum and end it.

No such luck. He saw Inka insert her fingers into Wava's dripping wet hole, finger fucking her and teasing her clit before withdrawing her hand, now wet with Wava's juices. Then he felt a light pressure on his left testicle. *What was she doing?*

Greg was already experiencing some very new sensations when he felt Inka gently push his testicle upward and into his body. He almost yelped but managed to turn his cry into a breathy gasp. Then Inka was sliding her finger into him, wearing his scrotum like a glove and fucking the opening where she had sequestered his left ball. The sensation was overwhelming. He wanted to squirm, but he was too afraid to move and jar Inka's finger out of place.

Greg should have known better. He tried to show up a pair of succubi and they were showing *him* parts of his body he didn't know were there. Inka was barely moving her finger, but it felt like he was being pounded by a power lifter. Meanwhile Wava continued to tongue fuck him while Sky's generous dick stretched his asshole to the limit.

Although Greg wasn't as enthusiastic as he was pretending to be, he could feel a climax building. There was no way to distract himself from this! He was going to cum soon. The hole Inka had found inside him was full of nerve endings. He could feel each tiny thrust of her finger firing off sensual sensations from the base of his dick to his asshole. Sky was barely moving but his cock was nestled tightly against Greg's prostate. Even with the odd sensation of his urethra being used, the combination of stimuli would make him cum before he could stop himself.

In a last-ditch effort Greg did the only thing he could do, "Cum with me Sky," he shouted, "I'm going to cum!"

Sky answered his prayer immediately and released a torrent of hot sperm into Greg, moaning with pleasure and relief. As soon as he felt Sky's ejaculate Greg grasped Inka's wrist with his left hand and pulled down to remove her fingers. With his right he pressed upward on Wava's forehead, to release his dick from her maw.

"We're done here!" Greg shouted, standing up and ignoring the hot stream of liquid flowing down the back of his thighs. Sky was lying back on the bed panting in ecstasy like Inka had been.

Wava and Inka released him without a fight, both of them laughing uproariously, "It's okay Greg, we'll go!" Inka said good-naturedly.

"Don't worry Greg, we weren't planning to double cross and kill you," Wava said easily.

"Or exsanguinate you," Inka added suspiciously.

Wava nodded, "I could never destroy you, my powerful little ass whore! I'm a connoisseur of the sexual arts and you are an *exquisite* bottom."

Greg blushed but said nothing.

Wava reached out her hand and took Greg's wrist, turning it over and using her claw to trace something onto his skin, "Call me if you want to finish what we started," she said with a giggle. Seconds later both demons disappeared with puffs of red and pink smoke. When he looked down at his wrist the number 666 was burned into his skin. Did they really *let* him win?

Greg grabbed another sports drink from the fridge and made his way back to Sky. Sky took it wordlessly, but their face was split with the biggest grin Greg had ever seen.

"What?" Greg said, annoyed in spite of his relief.

"Oh nothing," Sky said, clearly holding back laughter,

"I mean my boyfriend could fuck his way through the Necronomicon and come back alive, but I'd hate to brag!"

"Liar!" Greg said in mock accusation, pointing at his lover dramatically, "You *love* to brag!"

"You're right, my love, you're always right," Sky said sounding genuine, "I wouldn't *dare* start an argument because I know you'll win by the skin of your asshole!" They dissolved into laughter and this time Greg joined in. He couldn't wait to tell his therapist about *this*.

About The Author

Aspen Thorne

Aspen is a slutty trans masc from Oregon who loves to sell videos of his ass for cash. You may already know him from classics like "Worship at the Cathedral of Ass" or "Road trip to Beavertown". The Succubus Field Guide is his debut published work but it won't be his last. Keep an eye out for his upcoming novel, Lilith.

Praise For Author

"Best smut I've ever read and it's starring an ASEXUAL! I had no idea how much I needed this until I read it."

"A surprising lack of typos considering the author wrote this with one hand."

"I'll never forget the main character's asshole wrapping a dick like a present!"

"I laughed, I cried, I beat my meat. I never knew smut could take me on such an emotional journey but I loved every second of it!"

"First I devoured this story, then I devoured my husband's dick. He's never been more excited about me burying my nose in a book."

"Buy it for your wife!"

- ANONYMOUS READERS

Made in the USA
Middletown, DE
29 October 2022

13748243R00029